7|19

You're Perfect
the Way You Are!

Written by: Richard Nelson
Illustrated by: Evgenia Dolotovskaia

ISBN: 978-1-7752839-2-8

For Alexis,

I couldn't ask for a more perfect child!

"Good morning sweetie!"

Mom said, as she placed a heaping bowl of cereal in front of me.

"Do you think I have too many freckles?" I asked my older brother.

He looked away from his video game and said, "Yes... hahaha, I'm just kidding. No, you're perfect the way you are," and returned to his game as he continued to laugh at his joke.

"Is my nose too big?"
I asked my dolly.

From a distant room I heard somebody say,

"No, you're perfect the way you are."

"Am I too big Papa?" I asked as I sat on Grandfather's lap.

He smiled down at me and said, "You'll never be too big to sit on my knee. You're perfect the way you are."

"No, you're perfect the way you are!"
Everyone said at once.

"Are my feet too big?"
I asked my uncle who was working on his truck.

"Hahaha, no. I don't think so. You're perfect the way you are," he chuckled.

"Are my knees too bony?" I asked my mom.

She looked at them, smiled and said, "a little wrinkly now, but not too bony. But I don't know why you're concerned about your looks. You're perfect the way you are."

"No, you're not! You're perfect the way you are!"

I yelled down the hallway.

Mom was waiting by my bed, ready to tuck me in. "He's perfect the way he is," she agreed.

"And so are you.
Goodnight my perfect angel,"
were the last words I remember
hearing as I dozed off to sleep.

The End

Check out these other books by Richard Nelson.

AVAILABLE ONLINE AT AMAZON,
BARNES AND NOBLE,
AND OTHER VARIOUS ONLINE BOOKSTORES.

ALSO AVAILABLE AS AN E-BOOK.

Raised in Manitoba, Canada, Richard Nelson grew up in a family that loved to play games. As a child, Richard especially loved to play "what if" games, usually while helping out with the dishes. As he grew older, his love for exploring his imagination developed into a desire to create books for children.

If you'd like to be notified of new releases, or would like to see other books written by Richard Nelson, please visit our website at...

www.richardnelsonauthor.com

CPSIA information can be obtained
at www.ICGtesting.com
Printed in the USA
BVHW091112110619
550699BV00006B/36/P